For Oren and Coco. With heartfelt thanks to my story crew:
Rashin, Tara, John, Margot and Jackie — K.M.

To all innocent Syrian refugee children who have experienced horrible war and injustice
at a young age. Each has their own story, and they sail with their story boats
like messengers of hope and peace — R.K.

Text copyright © 2020 by Kyo Maclear
Illustrations copyright © 2020 by Rashin Kheiriyeh

Tundra Books, an imprint of Penguin Random House Canada Young Readers,
a Penguin Random House Company

Library and Archives Canada Cataloguing in Publication

Title: Story boat / Kyo Maclear ; [illustrations by] Rashin Kheiriyeh.
Names: Maclear, Kyo, 1970- author. | Kheiriyeh, Rashin, illustrator.
Identifiers: Canadiana (print) 20189069333 | Canadiana (ebook) 20189069341
ISBN 9780735263598 (hardcover) | ISBN 9780735263604 (EPUB)
Classification: LCC PS8625.L435 S76 2020 | DDC jC813/.6—dc23

Published simultaneously in the United States of America by Tundra Books of Northern New York,
an imprint of Penguin Random House Canada Young Readers, a Penguin Random House Company

Library of Congress Control Number: 2018966605

Edited by Tara Walker with assistance from Margot Blankier
Designed by John Martz
The artwork in this book was created with colored pencil and watercolor, oil and acrylic paint on painted paper, with
additional natural materials including wood, wool and cut paper.
The text was set in Charcuterie Serif.

Printed and bound in China

www.penguinrandomhouse.ca

1   2   3   4   5   24   23   22   21   20

Penguin
Random House
TUNDRA BOOKS

Story Boat

Words by **Kyo Maclear**

Pictures by **Rashin Kheiriyeh**

tundra

Here we are.

What's that?

Well, here is . . .

Here is just here.

Or here.

Here is a cup.
Old and fine, warm as a hug.

Every morning,
As things keep changing,
We sit wherever we are
And sip, sip, sip,
Sippy, sip, sip
Ahhhh
From this cup.

And this cup is a home.

Here is a blanket.
Patterned and soft, color of apricots.

Every night,
When the world feels not quite cozy,
And everyone seems weary
From hoping and hurrying,
We snuggle and dream
Under this blanket.

And this blanket is a sail.

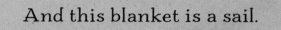

Here isn't always
the same.

Sometimes it's *here*
just for a moment.

Here is a lamp.
Big and bright, powered by the sun.

Every evening,
As the sky grows dark,
We write and read
And wonder, what will we be?
By the light of this lamp.

And this lamp is a lighthouse.

Here is a song that everyone can sing.
And *here* is the moon
And a million sparkling stars.

Here is a flower.
Bold and sweet, wild and welcoming.

Every day,
When the weather is nice,
Or gray and stormy,
We wonder, where will we be?
Who will we meet?
As we sit in the field
With these flowers.

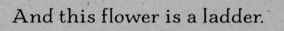

And this flower is a ladder.

Here is our journey
That holds the warmth of a cup,
The softness of a blanket,
The brightness of a lamp,
The strength of a flower
And the openness of a story.

Every week,
We dream and draw,
Make and play,
Search for treasure,
Find our way
And grow,
And wait
And wait
And wait
Adding words to this story.

And this story is a boat.

Here we are.

Here.